moose & goose
GO TO THE MOON

+ cat

Written by
Craig Westmoreland

Illustrated by
Mark Cullen

Acknowledgements

For my son and best friend, Ezra:

You're the one I wrote this book for
No-one else could love you more
Your eyes and smile, so big and bright
Make me want to hug you tight
Today you're young, but not forever
You will grow too, to be loving and clever
So with this book, Ezra I say
Thank you for being you, now and every day.

Your loving Dad

JoJo, Rachel, Mum and Dad

To my beautiful nephew, sister and parents,

Each day you are all in my thoughts
and in everything I do. Each of you has left your
own indelible mark on my life and I thank you.
Life will never quite be the same again, but the love
you have shown me will give me hope and strength
in the years ahead.

Your loving son, brother and uncle,

Mark

To Mark, friend, book Illustrator and co-author:

A show of thanks and a tip of the hat
For your drawing's of Goose, Moose and the lovely cat
Without you Mark, we'd have not got it done
For your talents and passion are second-to-none
You took on a vision and made it all right
So children can read our book out at night

Your friend, Craig

This is the story of a **BIG** friendly Moose,
He likes to adventure and **LOVES** his friend Goose.

One hot, summer's day, they talk of a **plan**,
To **venture** outside as **far** as they can.

They packed up their **lunch**, Moose searched for a **hat**,
And they set out for the day after feeding the **cat**.

They both crossed the road and strolled down the street,
To a clip, clippety-clop...

from the sound of their feet.

The pair kept on walking for mile upon mile,
Before taking a rest, they sat for a while.

"What's that by those rocks?" asked Goose up to Moose,
"It looks like a key – try twisting it loose".

With a wiggley wiggle and a wiggley weeeee,
They managed to loosen the big shiny key.

KEYS TO A ROCKET

It came with a key ring, a fine silvery locket,
Engraved with the words "KEYS TO A ROCKET"

So they boarded the **spaceship**, an epic contraption,
And strapped themselves in, all ready for **action**.

The duo were set, each in their place,
It was time for their mission to BLAST into SPACE!

With a twist of the key, a FLASH and a BOOOM.
The rocket set off, with a WHIZ and a ZOOOM.

In just a few **minutes**, not a moment too soon,
They glanced through the **window**,
They'd arrived on the **MOON!**

With a **CLUNK** and a **CLICK**, Moose opened the **door**,
They both peered **outside**, they were on the Moon's floor.

All that remained was a **small step** for Moose, but one **GIANT LEAP** for his little pal **Goose**.

Hopping and skipping, a jump and a leeeeap,
Goose and his friend were bounding like sheep.

They'd found a new **playground**, weightless and **fun**,
The only thing missing was **ice cream** and **sun**.

Both were amazed at how they **floated** with ease, as they dug lots of holes to find all the **cheese**.

They even made **friends** with an **alien** called ZOME.
But their time was now up, it was time to go **home**.

Zome said she would miss them, promised to write,
And if ever on Earth, would stay for a night.

Goose strapped himself in, a tear in his eye,
And shouted to Moose "It's time! We must fly!"

So they pointed at Earth with a cargo of cheese,
And the **rocket** set off with a **COUGH** and a **WHEEEEZE.**

They landed back safely, hip hip hooray,
Moose and his friend, content for the day.

The sun started **rising**, as they walked home **together**, To plan in more **memories** that would last them **forever**.

"But **where** will we **go**? **What** shall we **do**?"
"No matter my **friend**, as long as I have **you**."